The Blanket

John Burningham

CANDLEWICK PRESS
CAMBRIDGE, MASSACHUSETTS

When I go to
bed I always
take my blanket.

One night
I could not find
my blanket.

Mommy looked
in the bathroom.

Daddy looked
in the closet.

And I looked
under my bed.

But we could not
find the blanket.

So Mommy
looked in
the hamper.

And Daddy
looked in
the car.

But I found the blanket under my pillow and went to sleep.

Second U.S. edition 1994
First published in Great Britain in 1975
by Jonathan Cape Ltd., London by whose permission
the present edition is published.

Library of Congress Cataloging-in-Publication Data

Burningham, John.
The blanket / John Burningham.— 2nd U.S. ed.
Summary: Unable to find the blanket he always takes to bed with him,
a child enlists the aid of his family to help him look for it.
ISBN 1-56402-337-0
[1. Blankets—Fiction.   2. Lost and found possessions—Fiction.
3. Bedtime—Fiction.]   I. Title.
PZ7.B936Bl   1994
[E]—dc20   93-24288

2 4 6 8 10 9 7 5 3 1

Printed in Hong Kong

The pictures in this book were done in pastels, crayon, and ink.

Candlewick Press
2067 Massachusetts Avenue
Cambridge, Massachusetts 02140